THE WATSONS BEGINNINGS

The Watsons Beginnings

Arc One: Courtship & Marriage

A Prequel to *Refined and Returned*

Eireanne Michaels

Cover Art: "A Wet Sunday Morning" by Edmund Blair Leighton

Edited by Marijke Kriel

ISBN-13: 978-1-969841-04-0

First Print Edition, 2026

LITERARY REALMS PRESS

Disclaimer: This is a work of fiction. Unless otherwise indicated, all names, characters, businesses, places, events, and incidents in this book are either the product of the author's imagination or used in a fictitious manner. The author does not speak for or represent the people, companies, corporations, or brands mentioned in this book. While this work may incorporate historical figures and events, it is a dramatized interpretation and not intended as a factual account. Any characterizations, dialogue, or events are fictionalized for storytelling purposes.

Table of Contents

Preface

This story is a prequel to *Refined and Returned* by Eireanne Michaels, a completed version of *The Watsons*—the unfinished fragment by Jane Austen. Written on paper with watermarks from 1803 and 1804, *The Watsons* was set aside by Austen for reasons unknown and never completed. While many have speculated on why she abandoned it, the truth remains a mystery.

The original manuscript is preserved in:

MS. MA 1034, Morgan Library & Museum, New York

MS. Eng. e. 3764, Bodleian Library, Oxford

Eireanne Michaels has completed *The Watsons* by adhering to Austen's style, allowing her characters to act within the personalities Austen crafted. In developing the novel, the author created a detailed backstory for the Watson family, spanning three decades before the events of *Refined and Returned*. This prequel is part of that story.

Arc One:

Courtship & Marriage

This story is dedicated to—all those who have known fear, endured cruelty, and yet found the strength to trust and love again.

Prologue

The Watsons

The Reverend Robert Thomas Watson was the only son of Samuel Nottingham Watson, from an old Yorkshire family, and Margaret Davison, the daughter of Thomas Davison, Esquire, of *Blaikstone* in the same county.

Samuel had studied law and through his marriages increased both his fortune and his connections. His first wife, Miss Davison, brought a dowry of two thousand pounds and together they had three children: Robert, Theophila, and Susanna. Two years after Susie's birth, she and her mother both died in a smallpox epidemic. Samuel later married Miss Mordaunt, daughter of a Warwickshire baronet, who brought him another three thousand pounds and helped him gain a place in parliament at which time the family moved to London. Their only child, Penelope, was born before Robert's eleventh birthday, but her mother died soon after. Six months later, the family was in Yorkshire when Samuel married the widowed Mrs Turner, a cousin of his first wife with four thousand pounds. The couple had only one surviving child, Margaret, just a year and a half after Penny had been born.

The third Mrs Turner, being a distant relation as well as his step-mother, treated Robert as her own son, as did her father and brother, Misters William and Charles Turner whom he was bade to call "Grandfather" and "Uncle Charles". In 1757, William Turner inherited his family's estates, increasing his income exceedingly and enabling him to support Robert at Cambridge.

In 1762, while Robert was still a student, Theophila married Mr John Mordaunt; however, she passed away two years later in childbirth, leaving the family grief-stricken. Robert left university to mourn and never returned as he had already finished the courses he needed. He was ordained the following year and received the living under his "Grandfather's" patronage upon the retirement of the incumbent.

In 1768, Robert's father chose to step down from parliament due to health reasons. He then settled in Bath with his wife and daughters. It was there that he passed away in December the following year, but not until after Penelope met and married the wealthy Mr Francis Parker of *Lyndrygge* Manor in Devonshire.

Robert was deeply affected by his father's passing. While he shared many of his sire's physical traits, he was more reserved, and they often had clashing views on both religious and moral matters. However, he understood how much his father cared for him when the will was read. Samuel, knowing the living would not be enough for Robert to start his own family, and since all his daughters had inherited their mothers' fortunes, had left the whole of his wealth to his son. Robert offered to take in his step-mother and youngest sister, but they chose to remain in Bath. So, Mr and Mrs Parker, who had purchased a house on Pulteney Street, allowed the widow and her daughter to reside there.

Robert returned to Yorkshire alone. With a humble income of around one hundred and twenty pounds per annum plus the interest on his near three thousand pound inheritance in the four percents, he lived a very modest lifestyle. He managed his affairs prudently and even slowly increased his income through investments and improvements to his glebe lands. He was satisfied with his life, yet there were moments when he realized how isolated he was from his remaining family and loneliness set in.

The Willoughbys

The widowed Mrs Cassandra Beauclerk, née Willoughby, was the youngest of nine children born to a prominent family with several estates across England. Her father was the second son of Lord Middleton, and her mother was the sole heiress of *Briddhalh* Estate in Yorkshire.

By the time Cassandra was old enough to *come out* into society, her parents had both passed away. However, her eldest brother, Henry, had married the previous year, and he and his new wife became her chaperones. Cassandra was a very pretty girl, and, in her first season, attracted the eldest son of Lord Vere, who was himself the second son of a Duke. Her family was thrilled, and she married the Hon. Mr Beauclerk partly to please them and partly because such an advantageous marriage was sure to allow her to live in style.

However, the marriage was far from happy. Her husband was a drunkard and a gambler who frequented houses of ill repute. His reckless spending drained not only his fortune but also Cassandra's small dowry. When their union remained childless, she was unfairly blamed, and her husband began to show a darker side to his personality. Because of this, eight years later, when the Honourable Mr Beauclerk was found dead in the Thames one cold winter morning, she felt no grief—only relief for the end of her suffering.

Cassandra—now repulsed by the idea of marriage—returned to her family in Yorkshire to live out the rest of her days teaching her nieces to embroider poorly and read more than society deemed proper for young ladies.

Chapter One

New Acquaintances

Mr Watson

The Turner and Willoughby families were not quite neighbours. Their estates were upwards of forty miles from each other across the moors. However, they were both very influential families involved in parliament in North Riding; and both Henry Willoughby and Charles Turner, the only son of Mr William Turner of *Kyrkelidun*, were of a similar age and had attended Cambridge together from 1745. While one attended Jesus College and the other Trinity, the two schools were an easy distance and the two boys met as members of The Zodiac Club, which met infrequently at the Three Tuns—an Inn quite far from their colleges which made it easier to avoid being caught by their proctors. This common club led to a long friendship between the two young men. They often crossed paths again in Yorkshire's public sphere, sometimes as cordial rivals—both having served as High Sheriff of Yorkshire, and other times as allies at civic events.

Since his father's death, Robert Watson had been taken under the wing of his Grandfather Turner and Uncle Charles. In the spring of 1770, he was visiting York with the latter when they ran into Charles's friends. Turner introduced him, saying to the other man, "You remember my brother-in-law, the late Samuel Watson, no? This is his son, the Reverend Mr Robert Watson. I believe it is the first time you have met?"

They concurred, and Turner continued. "Robbie, this is my old schoolmate, Henry—Mr Willoughby to you. And this is his lovely wife and his sister," he paused for a moment to think, "Mrs Beauclerk, I do believe? It has been some time since we met, young lady," he said with a bow and a kiss over her hand.

She smiled, and Robert felt his heart skip a beat. "Sir, I believe we both know that, as a widow who was married for some years, I can no longer be considered a 'young lady'."

Robert could not account for the fluttering in his chest at the sight of Mrs Beauclerk, for the pang of sadness that came at hearing her referred to as a Missus, nor for the relief he felt when she said she was a widow. It was very wrong to feel thankful about the death of someone else's spouse, but he could not take his eyes off the lovely lady.

The rest of the party all spoke and laughed together which kept them from noticing Robert's discomfort. As a clergyman, he knew that he should not judge one on their appearance alone, but he was sure there was something about this woman. Her dark brown curls were peeking out from her matron's bonnet while her blue-grey eyes shone with good humour. She did not wear mourning colours, but he could still not be sure if he had any chance of winning her attentions.

She glanced at him as their companions spoke and offered him a smile before turning away again, but it was enough. Mr Robert Watson, at the ripe old age of twenty-nine, had felt Cupid's arrow for the first time in his life.

Mrs Beauclerk

Cassandra was the first of her party to see Mr Turner coming their way. She was about to call her brother's attention to his arrival when she was distracted by the man at his side. He was a good-looking, though not overly handsome, young man. His hair was a dark blonde, his eyes a honey-brown colour, and he was a tall, thin man—which contrasted with Mr Turner's slightly shorter and plumper frame.

He was soon introduced to them, and she found herself thinking that, for a clergyman who appeared near her own age, he was in surprisingly good shape and must spend a good deal of time exercising—perhaps to meet his parishioners? She considered this as she eyed him surreptitiously and noticed him watching her in return.

She decided to try and meet his gaze. Turning around, she did just that. She smiled at him and enjoyed the blush that quickly overtook his features. He swallowed hard but did not look away from her. She turned back to the conversation before she could no longer hold in her laughter. She had not spent much time in society before her marriage, and it was a new thing for her to leave a man so dazed in her presence before she had even had a chance to frighten them with her "independent thoughts" and "unconventional opinions".

She was not displeased to find she could still draw the notice of a handsome young man, yet she had no wish to encourage him; her late husband had left her with little regard for married life. Her family, friends, and indeed much of *the Ton* knew of his general activities when he was alive, but she did not inform them of his lesser-known habits.

Cassandra had been grateful when the lady's maid who had served her throughout her marriage agreed to take a lower-paying position to stay with her. Some of the wounds her husband had inflicted on her in his drunken rages would never fully heal, and she was glad that she would not have to expose her shameful past to another. Even though her maid insisted that she was not to blame, that it was to her husband's discredit, society believed otherwise.

No. The widowed Mrs Beauclerk had no intention of putting herself at the mercy of another man.

Mr Watson

When the two groups had separated in York, Turner had informed Robert that they would be needing to add an extra day to their journey as they had been invited to dine and stay the night at the Willoughbys' on their way home the following day.

As their carriage moved onto the lane leading to *Briddhalh* Manor, Robert wrung his hands in nervousness. He had never been good at speaking to women. Of course, he must speak with his parishioners—male and female of all ages—but that was different. Speaking to a woman whom one was attracted to was another matter altogether.

He was so lost in his musings that he didn't even notice Turner speaking to him until he heard the man's laughter and tore his eyes away from the window.

When Turner finally stopped chuckling, he asked, "Robert, dear boy, what has got into you? You act as if you are on the way to an inquisition. It is simply dinner at the house of a family friend." Turner stared at him as a slow smirk spread over his face. "Or is there a reason for your discomfort? A pretty young widow, perhaps?"

Robert was shocked. *Had he noticed? Had he seen Robert's feelings? Had the others? Had she?*

Turner laughed again at the fear showing on his face until Robert began to look chagrined. Then he leaned over and patted the younger man on the knee. "Fear not, my boy. Mrs Beauclerk is used to the admiration of others by now, I have no doubt. She is still an attractive woman—perhaps becoming more so with age, and it was such beauty which allowed her to marry so well in her first season. Had her husband survived, she would have one day been a baroness." He looked out the window at the house which was coming up quickly, and Robert listened eagerly for whatever else his Uncle Charles might share about the lady.

I fear that her marriage was not a happy one. Her husband's proclivities became well-known in London after their marriage." He was silent for a moment as they pulled up to the front of the house, and, before the door opened, he shook his head and said, "Thinking on it, I am afraid there is not much hope for you there, my boy."

Robert was confused about what he meant, but, as they exited the carriage and were introduced to the larger family party who met them outside, he thought over what was shared. When he greeted the lady in question, he took the chance to observe her more carefully. Cassandra had a lovely smile and a good sense of humour, but he thought he may have detected some reserve and melancholy in her eyes now that he got another look after hearing Turner's earlier comments.

Or was it simply his imagination?

Chapter Two

Dinner and Discussions

Mr Watson

They all sat around the parlour before dinner, and Robert learned that the Willoughbys had been in York to collect some of their visiting family and to make travel arrangements for the rest. He was surprised that Mr Willoughby would invite them to dine while all his family were gathered at his home and overwhelmed to meet so many people at once; nearly all of them were Willoughbys by name if not by birth.

Mr Henry Willoughby was the oldest of his brothers, but he and his wife accepted being called Mr and Mrs Henry in order to avoid too much confusion. They had four children; however, as they were twelve and under, they were only introduced to their parents' guests before being sent upstairs. Mr and Mrs Francis came next and were followed by the Reverend Mr James who was yet unmarried.

Their host then informed them, "Our youngest brother, Thomas, married the daughter of a baronet and purchased a small estate in Somerset, so he is unable to join us. He is the only one now who does not reside in Yorkshire since Cassandra returned upon her husband's death."

"I believe I remember hearing that Thomas married quite well, did he not? Is she not the daughter of a baronet?" questioned Turner.

Mr Henry laughed, "Indeed. One of the Musgrave girls—though there are so many of them that they none of them have much of a dowry to bring into marriage. However, the family is still an old and well-respected one, so the connection can only benefit him."

Robert noticed that most of the women of the party had ignored the conversation, but Mrs Beauclerk was clearly listening and cringed when they spoke of the Miss Musgrave in question as if her family's connections and fortune were her only assets. He only had a moment to consider this and what he knew about her before his host continued the introductions with his sisters' families. Apart from Mrs Beauclerk, the other three former Willoughby ladies had all married clergymen with positions in and around York.

The eldest daughter, Elizabeth—or Mrs Garforth, was the widow of a clergyman who now resided at *Briddhalh* with her young son, William; a strapping lad of eighteen who would be matriculating at Cambridge later that year. While the late Mr Garforth had left her a life-tenancy at his house in York, she chose to let the property after his death and reside with her brother.

"Eliza has been a boon to my dear wife and Cassie in giving them another companion when we are in the country," he added. "Nina and Emma do not reside much further than York; so, we are all able to come together at least once or twice a year."

Nina, or Antonina, was the wife of the Reverend Mr Hewgill while Emma was the wife of the Reverend Mr Hodgson. Both gentlemen held livings in Yorkshire, though the former was closer to *Kyrkelidun* than York.

Once they were all introduced, Turner joined Mr Henry and Mr Francis in political discussions while Robert found himself among the other clergyman who entered into their own debate. He sat back in his chair; his expression thoughtful as he listened to the conversation unfold. Mr Hodgson remarked about the duties of the clergy, and then Mr Hewgill, who had more traditional views, took up the thread.

"It is all very well to speak of duty," Mr Hewgill said, "but what is to be done when that duty is usurped? I was in Thirsk last month and heard of an itinerant preacher—one of these Methodists, no doubt—gathering crowds in the marketplace. Not a church in sight, and yet there he stood, proclaiming himself a shepherd to the flock. It is unseemly."

Mr Hodgson nodded but replied mildly, "It is hardly a new concern. John Wesley himself has preached in these parts, and his followers have only grown in number. Even in Richmond, I have seen them gathering in barns and outbuildings when no church would receive them."

Mr James, who had been listening with a hint of disapproval, cleared his throat. "But ought we not to be cautious? Too much descent leads to disorder. The Church was established for good reason, and those who stray beyond it risk more than their own souls."

Robert, who had remained quiet thus far, finally spoke. "I do not disagree with the dangers of unchecked zeal, but can we say the Church has done all in its power to guide these people? Many of them are poor labourers, men who toil on the moors or in the dales, rarely seeing their parson except on Sundays. They turn to these preachers because they speak to their needs in a way that sermons from the pulpit often do not."

Mr Hewgill frowned. "And what then? Shall we invite them into our churches and allow them to dictate our doctrines?"

"Not dictate," Mr Watson replied evenly. "But listen to them, perhaps. If a man seeks comfort in his faith, we should not scorn him for where he finds it. The Church must be strong, but it must also be a refuge."

There was a brief silence before Mr Hodgson smiled slightly. "A fair point, Mr Watson. It is easier to condemn than to instruct, but the latter serves the Church far better."

Mr James sighed, shaking his head. "Perhaps you are right. But I would still rather see a congregation gathered under the roof of a proper church than in a farmer's field."

Mr Hewgill grunted in agreement, but Mr Watson merely smiled. "As would I, sir. But if they seek us out elsewhere, we should not turn away from them."

Mrs Beauclerk

What Robert didn't know was that, as he spoke to her brothers, Cassandra sat among her sisters and listened to their nearby conversation. She was impressed by Mr Watson's open-mindedness and more modern views compared to the old-fashioned views of her brother and brother-in-law. She caught herself smiling with his final comments, and, when she was asked by her sisters what she found so amusing simply replied, "I am just enjoying such a delightful evening among good company. It has been too long."

Elizabeth gave her a knowing look which caused her to drop her smile. She had been miserable in her marriage and was intent on enjoying the freedom of being a widow, albeit one of little fortune, until the end of her days. While her husband had left her bereft of her dowry without even a small property to lease out for extra income like Eliza, she wasn't completely destitute. Her brothers had been able to pull together one thousand pounds to gift her in place of her lost dowry. It was not required of them, and she was most grateful for their care, but she also was glad it was not enough to tempt any man to try and compromise her freedom. She didn't want her family getting any ideas.

As she was over thirty, though still attractive, her brothers had agreed that she was likely too old to find a husband with so little monetary incentive and nearly no connections of note. Luckily, she was well-educated and would always have a place in her brother's house as long as she continued to help in teaching her nieces and nephews.

She was debating joining the ladies' conversation when the butler came in to announce dinner.

As everyone stood to move into the dining room, she inched her way towards Mr Watson in hopes that he would ask to be her escort. It was to be an informal arrangement, and, though she didn't wish to give the wrong idea, it had been a long time since she had anyone new and interesting to speak with. If she just happened to be nearest him when it was time to head into dinner, it could be passed off as mere happenstance.

Mr Watson

Robert was startled when he rose to join the throng heading into the dining room and discovered the object of his interest so near at hand—and still alone. He hesitated only a moment before she turned, meeting his gaze.

"Excuse me, my lady, but if you are not otherwise engaged this evening, might I offer you my escort?" he asked, his voice carrying a note of hope.

She gifted him with another of her radiant smiles and nodded, slipping her hand into the crook of his arm as he offered it. "Indeed, Mr Watson. I must admit that I was hoping you would ask."

His surprise left him in silent musings until they were both seated at the long table, but he could not miss the sly grin that curved at her lips every time she glanced at his perplexed visage.

He wondered aloud as the soup was served, "If I may ask, why were you hoping I would ask you?"

She chuckled lightly at the surprise in his voice. "Well, while it might not reflect well on me, I must admit that I was listening to your conversation earlier with my brothers."

She left him to think on this as she began to eat.

"And—may I ask—what you thought of our discourse?" he asked after a few bites.

She nodded, approving his acceptance that a woman might have her own thoughts and opinions on a man's conversation. "In fact, I quite agree with you. Not everyone has the means to attend services regularly. In remote areas, where the church is too far for those without the means to travel—especially in poor weather—it is understandable that parishioners might turn to any seemingly knowledgeable man who comes their way."

His only response at first was a raised eyebrow, and she wondered if she had said too much. Just then, the next dish was brought out.

"It is not often that I meet a woman interested in such matters," he said once the servants had moved away.

She was about to take umbrage when he continued in the same composed manner, "Do you have any thoughts on how the clergy might better serve their more distant parishioners?"

She looked at him in disbelief, but as she met his gaze, her surprise turned to something else entirely—genuine astonishment at the honest curiosity in his expression.

She tilted her head, considering him. "Are you certain you wish to ask me that? You may find that once a woman is allowed to express an opinion, she has many more to share."

His lips twitched, but he inclined his head in encouragement.

"Well then," she continued, her tone turning more thoughtful, "perhaps the clergy might take a lesson from those itinerant preachers they so disdain and travel to their distant parishioners rather than expecting them to come to the church. A sermon delivered in a barn or a village square may not have the dignity of a pulpit, but it would at least be heard."

She watched for his reaction, half-expecting resistance, but instead, he merely nodded, his expression contemplative.

"You would have us take the church to the people," he said. "A radical notion indeed, but not without merit. I have considered the option myself."

She smiled, pleased to see that he was truly considering her words. "You see? A dangerous thing, asking a woman for her thoughts."

He smiled back at her, "On the contrary, I see nothing wrong with it. After all, any clergyman worth his weight must learn to listen to both sexes in order to truly provide the necessary care to his flock."

His words took her aback, but she was impressed to say the least. They continued on throughout the dinner, all but ignoring the other diners, and neither of them noticed the sly looks they received from her family and his.

If Cassandra *had* noticed the looks exchanged by her brothers, she might have realized that she was the only one who considered herself off the market.

Chapter Three

An Unconventional Courtship

Omniscient

Though they lived quite far from each other making it hard to meet, especially on Robert's limited income, he used every chance he could to visit Cassandra. Whenever his uncle had business in York—which happened every few weeks to every other month—Robert would make an excuse to join him. On those visits, they were nearly always invited to visit the Willoughby estate, and he spent almost every moment in Cassandra's company.

While the visits were infrequent, Cassandra always found herself looking forward to the next meeting. His interest in her thoughts and opinions never waned, and she found them speaking of everything from lace and ribbons—as he had grown up with three younger sisters and had learned enough to hold his own, which greatly amused her—to politics. They also made book recommendations for each other.

Robert suggested histories such as Tobias Smollett's *A Complete History of England* and David Hume's *The History of England*, which led to lively discussions comparing their differing styles and views. He also proposed biographies like Samuel Johnson's *The Life of Richard Savage*. Meanwhile, Cassandra introduced him to the more controversial novels of the time, including Sarah Fielding's *The Adventures of David Simple*, Oliver Goldsmith's *The Vicar of Wakefield*, and her personal favourite, Charlotte Lennox's *The Female Quixote*.

One fine summer day when the *Briddhalh* Willoughbys visited as the guests of the Turners at *Kyrkelidun* Hall, Robert invited Cassandra for a walk about the gardens. As they wandered along the gravel path, Cassandra slowed to admire the soft hues of the ripening apples and the flowers that decorated the large park in neatly divided sections. Beyond the trimmed hedges, the gentle murmur of conversation drifted from the gazebo, where the others sat enjoying tea.

"I must say, I found Smollett's *History of England* rather engaging," she remarked. "He writes with such spirit—one cannot help but be swept up in his narrative."

Robert gave a knowing smile. "That is my complaint. He does not present history so much as wage a war upon it. Every monarch is either a hero or a villain, with no room for anything in between."

She tilted her head. "And you would prefer Hume's impassive detachment? His '*history*' reads as though he were dissecting events with a scalpel rather than telling a tale of kings and nations."

Robert chuckled. "Perhaps that is why I admire him. He allows the reader to form their own conclusions. A historian should not be a dramatist."

"But history *is* drama," she countered. "It is not merely a sequence of events—it is the clash of ambitions, the rise and fall of empires. Smollett *feels* history."

"And Hume *understands* it."

She laughed. "So, you dismiss passion in favour of reason?"

"I prefer moderation," he said with a shrug. "A historian should not impose his feelings upon the past, just as a clergyman should not perform in the pulpit. Theatrics may stir the emotions, but they do little to inspire true reflection. Historians, like clergymen, should not harangue the audience or try to sway them, but should simply tell the facts as they are and allow for interpretation."

Cassandra considered this as they strolled past a row of budding lilacs, and she leaned in to take in the scent. Robert could not help but think to himself, as he gazed upon her with admiration, how well she fit in among the flowers. When she returned to his side, she said, "Then you must think me terribly misguided in my preference for Smollett."

He looked at her with amusement and chuckled again. "Not misguided. Merely fond of a good story. But tell me—if you were to write a history, which style would you prefer?"

She smiled. "Why, neither. I would write a novel."

Robert laughed out loud at her impertinence. "Of course you would."

A couple weeks later, Robert was again visiting Mr Willoughby's estate when heavy rains trapped him and his uncle there for two days. During this time, he and Cassandra spent long hours walking the galleries as she shared stories of her family's history or retreating to the library, where their shared love of books filled the quiet hours.

Sometimes, they simply sat together on the settee, each absorbed in their own reading, content in one another's company as their chaperones exchanged bemused glances at the unspoken courtship unfolding before them. Other times, they read aloud to each other, pausing now and then to discuss a passage or share a particularly striking scene from their chosen works.

The steady patter of rain against the tall windows filled the library, a gentle, rhythmic backdrop to Cassandra's voice as she finished reading aloud the final passage of *The Female Quixote*. She closed the book with a satisfied sigh and set it aside on the small table between them. Across from her, Robert sat in the deep armchair, one leg crossed over the other, his expression thoughtful.

"Well?" she prompted, tilting her head slightly. "You have listened to every word—have I converted you into an admirer of Arabella?"

Robert exhaled a quiet laugh, shaking his head. "I will admit to admiring her tenacity. And I can see why you favour the book—there is a certain cleverness to the way Lennox exposes the absurdities of romantic delusions. But I cannot say I envy any man who should have the misfortune of reasoning with such a lady."

Cassandra's lips curled into a teasing smile. "Ah, but you see, that is precisely why I adore her! She has such conviction, such unwavering faith in her own understanding of the world. It is delightful to watch everyone about her flounder under the weight of her certainty."

Robert leaned forward slightly, resting his forearms on his knees. "But does she not weary you? Her obstinacy is rather trying."

Cassandra shrugged. "Perhaps a little, but only because she takes so long to see reason. And yet, I find her a more compelling character than David Simple."

Robert nodded at that, settling back against the chair. "He is sincere to a fault, but his story is a rather grim reflection of human nature. The world is unkind to the honest man who seeks only friendship."

Cassandra sighed, glancing at the rain-streaked window. "Yes, and though Fielding's tale is meant to be sentimental, I find it almost tragic. David Simple wants goodness, but he does not understand how rare it truly is. He never learns to guard himself against the selfishness of others."

Robert tapped a finger against the arm of his chair. "That is why I think Goldsmith's Dr Primrose is the more successful character. He suffers misfortune after misfortune, yet he never loses faith in virtue. And unlike David, he is rewarded for it in the end."

Cassandra turned back to him, eyes alight with amusement. "But do you not find him rather absurd? You praised *The Female Quixote* for exposing delusions, and yet Dr Primrose is hardly less foolish in his unwavering optimism."

Robert chuckled. "That is true. But I suppose I prefer a fool who finds happiness in the end over one left wandering in disappointment."

She considered this, then inclined her head. "I can see the appeal in that."

For a moment, they sat in companionable silence, the warmth of the library and the soft rain outside enclosing them in a world of quiet thought. Cassandra traced the leather spine of *The Female Quixote* with a finger before glancing up at him once more.

"You must allow me to choose your next novel," she said with mock seriousness. "I think you need something with a little more adventure."

Robert raised a brow. "And in return, may I subject you to yet another history?"

Settling back into her chair, she let out a long sigh as if about to take on a large burden. "If you must then there is nothing to be done about it." They both laughed at her concession.

And so, in the quiet library, while their chaperones lingered just out of earshot, the rain continued to fall, and an unspoken understanding settled between them, woven not in words, but in books shared and silences comfortably kept. They had no idea about the conjectures being made by their respective families on how soon the couple would join them into one, and they would have very different opinions on the concept when they learned of it.

Chapter Four

A Sister's Counsel

Mrs Beauclerk

It had been some time since Cassandra had left *Briddhalh* even to visit with her other siblings. She had spent the last couple of years rotating between Henry, Hodgson, and Hewgill's homes; however, recently she preferred to remain at *Briddhalh*—just in case Mr Watson should call.

A few days after the rain had stopped and he had left them again, Cassandra was assisting her sister Elizabeth in the stillroom. Mrs Henry Willoughby had been with them, but she had been called away by the housekeeper to discuss a matter with the grocer's bill. The two sisters kept on with their work, and Cassandra was surprised when Elizabeth suddenly changed the topic of their conversation.

"Will you not be visiting Nina or Emma anymore this summer? I had thought you might be wanting to make a trip to York for some shopping."

Cassandra only glanced at her sister curiously before turning back to the flowers and herbs she was preparing. "You know that I have very little pin money to waste on fripperies even should I enjoy looking around the shops. What caused you to ask all of a sudden? Do you feel that I have been neglecting our sisters?"

"Oh, it is just that I was speaking with our brother and sister about it only yesterday. We were all surprised when you declined his invitation to ride to town on the morrow. I daresay you will be wanting some new clothes—or at least a few new night things—soon. So, it only seemed reasonable that you would wish to purchase them in York if given the chance."

Cassandra laughed though taken aback. "Will I? It has only been four years since Vere's death, and you were all kind enough to help me purchase new clothes when I came out of mourning. Are my gowns already so dowdy?"

Elizabeth gave her a knowing glance. "I was only thinking that Mr Watson should be making you an offer soon." She missed the flash of panic that crossed her sister's face as she turned back to her work. "Your courtship has already lasted several weeks, and it is not as if you are growing any younger. He will be good for you, and both Henry and Hodgson are excited for the connection though for different reasons. According to Emma, Hodgson even asked me to send on his request that you bring Mr Watson by from time to time. He has been pleased to have an accomplice in combating James and Hewgill's old-fashioned beliefs."

She laughed at the thought, but when Cassandra did not reply, she turned to look at her sister and was shocked by what she saw.

"Cassie! You are white as a sheet! Come, come, sit down here." Cassandra had begun shaking and hyperventilating at the thought of being subjected to another marriage. Elizabeth had no idea what had affected her sister, but she led Cassandra over to a stool and helped her sit. "Wait there," she said before hurrying to call for some restorative tea.

When she returned, Cassandra looked less pale but no less anxious. Elizabeth allowed her time to sip her tea in silence while she finished hanging the herbs to dry. At last, when her task was complete, they moved to the parlour to speak more comfortably.

Elizabeth waited to speak until the downstairs maid had brought them more tea and a tray of cakes and biscuits before leaving them alone once more. "Now, take this," she said, handing Cassandra a new cup of freshly brewed tea along with a small cake. "And tell me what that was all about just now."

Cassandra ate the cake slowly, using the time to gather her thoughts. She knew that she was completely uninterested in the idea of remarriage, but she could not account for the sudden and strong fear that had enveloped her at the very thought. She had suddenly remembered scenes, vivid scenes of *his* cruelty, that she had thought were all in the past.

When she could no longer stall, she began, "You—you know something of the issues with my marriage and my late husband."

Her sister nodded but said nothing, allowing her to continue.

Cassandra took a deep breath, and in a near whisper said, "The truth is, it was much worse than what is generally known."

Elizabeth's eyes flew open; however, before she could ask anything, Cassandra raised a hand to stop her.

"I am not ready to talk about it," she said firmly. "My maid knows my reasoning and has helped me keep the secret all this time. I do not know why I am even telling you this much but—" she paused as her breathing had once again become laboured. She sipped at her tea until she calmed while her older sister looked on with mingled horror and pity. Cassandra did not like to see either expression, but she was used to much worse on the face of her poor lady's maid. "The truth is, I swore to myself that once I was free of his power, I would never again put myself at the mercy of another man. Even thinking about it—" she convulsed at the thought and almost spilled her tea. "I—I cannot," she said in a whisper though there was a conviction in her voice.

Silence settled between them for some time as Elizabeth considered how to respond to such a confession. While her sister had not told her any details, her physical reaction added to what little she *had* said was enough for her to get an idea of what Cassandra had suffered—was *still* suffering. As a clergyman's wife, she had seen women living in all sorts of circumstances; she knew what some women were forced to endure if their husband was not a good man.

She soon gasped with realization, "Is that—is that why you always insist on wearing long sleeves?" She could not help the sob that came out with the last word.

Cassandra only nodded with tears now streaming quietly down her face. Elizabeth threw her arms about her sister and the two sat weeping in each other's embrace for some time.

When they had both finally calmed down enough to speak, Elizabeth asked her sister in a slow and careful tone so as to not upset her sensibilities once more, "Then you will not consider Mr Watson's suit?"

Cassandra shook her head. "I cannot." It pained her to say it as she had grown to care for him deeply, but had she not once cared for *that man* as well? And how could she even consider what came with marriage? The idea of Robert seeing the scars that marred her skin, of explaining their origin, of admitting to what she had experienced.

"I have suffered too much already. I am now old enough—and poor enough—to enjoy some small independence and avoid another such risk."

"But you love him, do you not?" her sister asked in a near whisper. "Can you honestly tell me you do not care for him?"

"Of course, I care for him!" Cassandra exclaimed even as her tears began anew. "How could I not do so? He is the kindest, most open-minded man I have ever known. He listens to my thoughts and ideas, and I am greatly mistaken if he does not also enjoy hearing them. He is a good friend, and if only—" She choked on a sob. "If only—" she covered her face with her hands and began to weep again.

"If only you had met him first?" Mrs Garforth finished for her as she calmly patted her dear little sister's back in a soothing gesture.

It was too much. Cassandra's sobs turned to wails, and Elizabeth embraced her little sister once more. They did not hear the knocking that preceded the entrance of Henry who had just returned from business with his steward, and Cassandra was unaware of both the apprehension on his face and of Elizabeth's quietly shooing him away.

While Elizabeth could scarcely imagine what her youngest sister had endured, she could only regret that their father had not lived long enough to protect her from it in some way. Yet she did not want Cassandra to turn away from what might be her best chance at happiness. She must try to help her sister to overcome her fear and give Mr Watson a chance, for she was sure that he was a very different sort of man and would never harm Cassandra in either body or mind.

"My dear," she murmured once Cassandra's wails had subsided, "I hate to see you like this. But I hope you will not dismiss him just yet."

Cassandra looked up in shock and began to pull away as if struck.

"Hear me out, Cassie." Her voice was soft but her tone was unyielding. "You *love* him—do not deny it. It is as clear as day to anyone who sees you together." She paused to let that sink in. "You must know that you love him."

Cassandra's expression flickered between anger and chagrin. "I know. I also know that he is not—"

"Yes," her sister interrupted, "You know that he is *nothing* like that man, but you will not accept it. Mr Watson is truly a good and honourable gentleman. You have seen it for yourself—you have said it for yourself. What if—what if God placed him in your path to give you a chance at happiness, Cassie? And just think of Mr Watson, whose love for you has been plain from the start. Are you truly willing to break his heart for the sake of a man long dead? Are you willing to let him marry someone else while you wither away at our brother's estate—caring for his children instead of having your own?"

Cassandra flinched. "But I cannot—I cannot have children."

"Says who? Hush. I know what they say, but these things are not always the woman's fault. Remember Mrs Jamison? She was married eight years and never felt the quickening, yet with her second husband she had twelve healthy offspring—the last when she was six-and-forty. And even if you cannot have children, what of the rest? What of your happiness?"

Cassandra said nothing, but Elizabeth could see that she was at least considering the idea. That was enough for now.

"You do not need to answer me today. After all, he has not yet asked anything of you. I only hope—" she lifted Cassandra's chin with her finger so that their gazes met, "that you will not reject the idea without truly considering what it is you would be giving up."

Cassandra held her eyes for a long moment before nodding, and the two of them silently returned to their rooms as it was past time they began preparing for dinner.

Chapter Five

Reflections and Resolutions

Mrs Beauclerk

That night, Cassandra lay awake for hours, her mind turning over memories of Robert and her late husband—comparing them, weighing them, trying to reason with herself.

Robert was kind. He was thoughtful. He listened to her, not just out of politeness, but because he valued her thoughts. He sought out her company, not to control her, but because he enjoyed it. She never felt afraid of what he might say or do. If she disagreed with him, he debated with her, never dismissing her words. If she was upset, he noticed. He did not push, only offered comfort in whatever way she would allow.

Her husband had known how to act kind, too. In public, he had been charming, affable—even doting. But she had learned quickly how little that meant once they were alone. He drank too much. Gambled away money they didn't have. Lied so effortlessly she had often doubted her own mind. And when he was in a temper, she had known better than to speak. Better than to look at him the wrong way. Better than to hope for gentleness.

Cassandra curled into herself, the old fear twisting in her stomach. She had been so young then. She had not known how to protect herself—she had had no power to do so. And in the end, when he had died, people had pitied her for being left alone, as if that had been the tragedy. They had never understood that his death had been her only freedom.

She pressed a hand over her mouth, swallowing the sob that rose in her throat.

Robert was not that man. He would never be that man. She knew this. She knew it. But how could she ever trust a man again? How could she be certain?

And even if she could—if she dared to hope for happiness—what of him? He deserved a wife who could give him everything: security, love, and children. She could give him nothing but herself, and she feared that, in the end, it would not be enough.

It was fortunate that Elizabeth had pointed out the nearness of Mr Watson's proposal, giving Cassandra time to think and make her decision before it actually happened, for it was only one week later that she found herself once again in Robert's company. Two days after that fateful conversation, she had resolved to avoid him by following through on a months-old promise to visit the Hodgsons, who lived very near to York.

As it happened, Robert and Mr Turner were in the city around the same time, and they diverted their trip home to call at the Hodgsons. This was easily done, as Mr Hodgson had long since offered Mr Watson a standing invitation, hoping to converse with him again. Cassandra was shocked to see her plan to escape him turn so completely against her.

Cassandra was exhausted from the haunting nightmares of her past relationship. Therefore, she could not muster the same energy to speak with him as she had before. Robert asked about her health and encouraged her to rest indoors, but she had insisted on taking a walk which led to her accompanying her sister in giving him a tour of the rectory's gardens.

Soon after their walk began, the Hodgsons' housekeeper appeared and called her sister away, leaving Cassandra alone with Mr Watson. She felt both nervous and excited, and began to shake as fear overcame her. She had tried to prepare herself for this moment, but now that it was here, she felt her heart waver.

He did not comment on her trembling—if indeed he noticed it through his own nervousness—when he began, "While I know it is improper for us to be alone together, I cannot let such a chance pass me by. Mrs Beauclerk, you must.

allow me to tell you how ardently I admire and love you. It has been some time since I became enamoured with your mind and your opinions. While it was your beauty that first attracted me, it was our diverting conversations and shared views that made me realise how strong my attachment had become."

Cassandra listened but could not respond, and he continued with hope in his eyes.

"Mrs Beauclerk—Cassandra, if you will allow me to call you that—I would be the happiest man on earth if you would accept my feelings and agree to become my wife and helpmeet, that we might spend the rest of our lives sharing our thoughts and opinions together. While I cannot offer you much, I have just over three thousand pounds—closer to thirty-two hundred, in fact—and my present living provides another one hundred and forty pounds per annum on top of the interest. While I know you are accustomed to a less humble lifestyle, I hope you will at least consider the happiness I can bring you."

He had been fumbling with his hat in his hands for some time, and she feared he might tear through it entirely. The thought was oddly calming, and she found her voice at last.

"Mr Watson," she began quietly, "I thank you for your honesty, and I am humbled by your affections for me."

She saw his smile fade into confusion, and turned her eyes just past him so she would not have to watch the grief she was about to cause.

"I am afraid that my previous experience in marriage has left me with no love for the institution. I have no intention of ever remarrying. While I deeply respect you and have greatly enjoyed all our conversations and debates, and would be happy to keep up a friendship if you are willing, I have no interest or intention of marrying anyone. It is not about your fortune—though mine is part of the problem. My late husband left me with nothing, and the little I have now was a gift from my siblings to give me some small independence. I cannot bring a fortune into our marriage, nor the connections that might aid you in the church, nor can I provide you with children, for in my previous marriage I never once felt the quickening. Because I care for you and respect you, I wish you to have the chance to find someone who can give you everything you deserve in life."

He tried to interrupt and tell her he did not need any of that—that he wished only for her companionship—but she held up her hand to stop him.

"My answer is final, and I am sorry if it pains you. If we cannot be friends after this, I will understand, but I hope you will also understand my position. I will not again be placed in the power of any man."

With that, she turned and hastened away. Once she was out of sight, her tears could no longer be held back, and they fell freely. She did not hear the sound of pursuit, but wished only to reach her room as soon as possible, so she quickened her steps.

On her way, she passed her sister Emma who was returning to join them. Emma tried to stop her and ask what was wrong; however, Cassandra only waved her off, telling her that she didn't feel well. She reached her room, locked the door, and turned away anyone who came to see her.

Even after she heard the carriage taking their guests away, she refused to go downstairs. She sent a maid with a note to her sister, asking that supper be sent to her rooms and that she be allowed her isolation for the remainder of the day. If this was acceptable, she promised to explain everything in the morning.

That night, the sleep that should have been restful was anything but. Cassandra tossed and turned in the dark, the images from her dreams a blur of old horrors. *He* was there again—looming in the shadows. The sound of *his* voice echoed in her mind—words sharp and filled with disdain, followed by the familiar, hollow thud of her body hitting the floor. The memory of *his* hands, cold and forceful, haunted her thoughts like a spectre she couldn't shake.

She woke with a jolt, her heart pounding in her chest, drenched in sweat. The room was dark and silent, but the echoes of her past clung to the air. Her breath came in shallow gasps, as though her body could still feel *his* presence, even now.

The past was never far. Every time she closed her eyes, she could almost hear the drunken slur of *his* accusations, could feel the weight of *his* rage bearing down on her, could taste the sharp bitterness of *his* words and the blood in her mouth. She had wanted to scream, to fight back, but the terror had always frozen her in place. The terror of not knowing when it would stop—or if it ever would.

Her chest ached from repressed emotions, but she steadied her breathing, as if willing herself to remain grounded in the present. *Robert is not that man*, she told herself. But the reminder felt too weak, too fragile, against the flood of memories she couldn't escape.

"What was that all about yesterday, Cassandra?" asked Emma over breakfast the following day. "I thought you enjoyed Mr Watson's company. Has anything happened that I should know of?"

While she felt guilty about her rejection of—and subsequent escape from—Robert's company, she couldn't bear to see his disappointment. She realized just how much time she often spent thinking about him and wishing for his company.

The night before, Cassandra had paced her room—the thought of meeting Robert again made her chest tighten with uncertainty. She had promised herself she would avoid him—she would act as she always had before; however, the thought of him looking at her differently, avoiding her, hating her—she had already begun to miss their camaraderie.

The memories of how, every time they met, his eyes had softened. How, when they had spoken, he had truly listened to her thoughts. How, for the first time in years, she had felt truly seen and appreciated. It had all come unbidden to her mind as she tried to stop thinking of him. She had remembered the way he always smiled without pretence, and how she had laughed freely in his company with no fear that he would suddenly lash out at her.

Robert had seen her—truly seen her, and it had made her feel cherished—yet vulnerable.

With each thought, a weight had settled deeper in her chest. She had squeezed her eyes shut, as if to shut out the memories, but they had only grown clearer in her mind's eye—the warmth of his gaze, the sound of his voice, the tenderness of his touch. She feared it was all just wishful thinking.

Hope was a dangerous thing, was it not?

Back in the present, she felt the tears welling in her eyes and excused herself from the table; leaving a baffled Mr and Mrs Hodgson behind. She burst out of the house and into the gardens where she proceeded to pace about. Her arms moved almost as constantly as her feet; she wrapped them around herself as if she could hold all the emotions inside before flinging them upward to grasp her head—wishing to tear off her bonnet and all these unmanageable thoughts and memories with it.

The thoughts of Robert's kindness, so different from everything she had experienced before, felt like both an invitation and a threat. She loved him, but she was scared. She wanted to be with him, but she craved her independence. Suddenly, an image of their happy future, though childless, passed through her mind. The two of them walking through the autumn leaves to visit the parishioners. Them sitting together by the fireplace, reading to each other in the winter. Robert accompanying her on walks through his uncle's gardens as their family chatted happily nearby. And summer days much like the ones they had already shared, but the difference was that there would no longer be a need for goodbyes.

It was during this lull in her storm of emotions that she heard her sister's voice calling her back to reality.

"What on earth has happened, Cassie? You look a sight!" Emma exclaimed as she came upon her and saw the state of Cassandra's bonnet.

Cassandra could say nothing more than, "Oh, Emma! Em! What have I done?" before throwing herself into her sister's arms and relating the whole of her ordeal through sobs and tears.

Chapter Six

Proposals of Marriage

Mrs Beauclerk

Cassandra was once again in her brother Henry's carriage, travelling with him. However, this time, they would only break their journey at *Briddhalh* and would be continuing on to *Kyrkelidun* after a day's rest.

When she had finally opened up to her sister Emma, she still had not told her of everything she had experienced, but, like with Elizabeth, she had told her enough to understand why Cassandra had made the decision she had. However, she had also explained all of her conflicting feelings. Emma had insisted that Cassandra share at least her general fears and anticipations with Mr Hodgson, since, "as a clergyman, he dealt with people from varying walks of life, and who had been through varying experiences, and could likely give better advice than Emma herself."

So, the three of them had spent the next few days discussing. Though they did not force any decisions on Cassandra, the Hodgsons had tried to help her work through some of her latent fears, as well as her feelings towards Mr Watson. After nearly a se'nnight, she had finally accepted the truth—that she did not wish to live her life without Robert. And, with that decision, she had written to her brother Henry, requesting him to pick her up at his earliest convenience in York.

Mr and Mrs Hodgson had taken her to the inn and stayed with her until Henry came to collect her. They had explained the gist of what happened, and, while he had been utterly flabbergasted at Cassandra's refusal of Mr Watson, once he had learned about her fears and their cause, he had nearly flown into a rage in the middle of the inn. Luckily, Mr Hodgson had been prepared to calm him and reminded him that "the perpetrator had already received retribution and his judgment from the good Lord."

Though this had not assuaged Henry's anger, it had allowed him to calm himself to the extent that he was able to continue the conversation. He had quickly agreed with Cassandra's plan of travelling to Kyrkelidun. *However, he had been curious what she planned to do once she got there.*

He had pointed out, "My dear Cassandra, while Mr Watson is a very reasonable and intelligent young man, it is hard to believe that after such a refusal, even as kind as you were in your wording, that he would wish to see you again so soon. Perhaps we should give him some time."

Cassandra had admitted that she considered the same. "However, it is exactly because I hurt him that I wish to remedy the situation as soon as possible. I do not wish to leave him alone to stew on the rejection until it can ruin his opinion of me."

At this, Henry had laughed, shocking them all. "Oh, my dear Cassandra, I do not think there is anything that could change Mr Watson's opinion of you. After all, he is the only man I know who could stand up to your strong, opinionated mind—and your honesty in expressing it."

As they sat in the carriage going down the bumpy lane, she enjoyed the views of the Moors as much as she had on their previous visit. However, this time there was some feeling of fear and anticipation. She was still worried that a man once refused would not be willing to renew those sentiments, and it was with that heaviness upon her that she alighted from the carriage with the aid of her brother.

When Mrs Henry Willoughby had heard of her sister-in-law's plight two days earlier, she had lamented with her, but also insisted on coming along. For all of her family was sure that Robert could not possibly refuse her and would be sure to renew his sentiments.

When they arrived, only Mr William Turner and his son, Mr Charles Turner, were there to greet them at the door. They informed them that, due to the nature of Henry's note to Charles, the latter had decided not to inform Robert of their arrival. This created even more fear in Cassandra as she could not be sure how he would react upon seeing her. However, Charles noticed the look on her face and assured her, "Oh, do not worry. He has been moping about for days ever since your refusal of him."

At her shock, he laughed outright. "Oh, yes, I have heard about it, but do not worry. I warned him before he began his courtship that you might not be willing to enter into another engagement. However, he would try his luck, and it seems it was not entirely a wasted effort." He then winked at her, making her blush. However, it did not stop the trembling of her hands as they were led into the house to clean up and rest before they must prepare for dinner, when she would be able to see Robert again—though hopefully not for the last time.

After their rest and preparations for dinner were complete, they went downstairs to join the family in the parlour as they awaited Mr Watson's arrival. When he came, he showed a strong look of surprise; his greeting to her was warm but cautious. After his polite inquiries as to her health and recent doings, he moved over to her brother and Mr Charles Turner, leaving Cassandra with her sister-in-law.

When they moved into dinner, it was her brother who offered his arm, as their host had escorted his wife to the dining room. Though she looked to Robert, he had his back to her and was moving into the dining room with Mr Charles, causing her heart to sink.

Over dinner, conversation was light and sociable, yet she never had the chance to speak privately with Robert. The same occurred after dinner, and she was starting to lose hope.

However, the next morning she woke with new determination. She asked Mr Charles if he could arrange a private meeting between her and Robert. He grinned and bowed. "Your wish is my command, my lady," which made her laugh, though she was still nervous.

It was later that afternoon when she, along with Mr and Mrs Henry Willoughby, were taken by Mr Charles to see the parsonage where Robert lived. Robert had clearly been given some warning of their arrival and was at the door to greet them. He seemed abashed to be showing them around his "small abode," as he called it, though the house itself was quite lovely.

In the front, there were neatly trimmed bushes and a row of colourful flowers. To the side, a large vegetable patch was kept in perfect order. Behind the house, a wooded area could be seen; they were informed that part of it was on the parsonage's property and helped him save money on coal, as he could cut timber when needed.

At one point, Robert left the party in the parlour in order to speak with his housekeeper. During his absence, the rest of the guests suddenly felt a strong interest in seeing the vegetable garden again. Cassandra smiled, especially after receiving winks from both gentlemen as they slipped quietly away.

When Robert returned, there was a flicker of apprehension in his eyes before he quickly offered to go and find the others. She stopped him at once. "No, that will not be necessary. In fact, if you are willing—which I hope you are—I would like a moment to speak with you alone."

He nodded slowly and stepped into the room, taking a seat farther from her than she would have liked. She understood his caution—and the impropriety of being alone—but as a widow of experience, she did not think such strict adherence to social etiquette need stand between them.

"I have some apologies to make to you," she said. She then apologised for her earlier refusal, and, not knowing how long they might have together, told him that if all went well, God willing, she would one day explain everything that had led to it. For now, she could only say that "her first marriage had left her with mental and emotional scars, as well as physical ones" before she paused, watching a succession of emotions cross his face—confusion, horror, anger—and she feared he might react as her brother Henry had. She realized that she was not afraid of his anger, but she was afraid for his peace of mind. Before such an outburst could happen, she continued quickly, "It was a long time ago, and, while I may never fully recover, I want to try."

He stared at her for a long moment, and she thought she saw light returning to his eyes. "I rejected you because I feared ending up in the power of another man—a man like my late husband. That was wrong of me. It was cruel to compare you with him, even for a moment, for you are nothing alike. In truth, you are nearly his opposite, which is what drew me to you in the first place—your intelligence, your kindness, your open mind, your willingness not only to allow me opinions of my own but to listen to them, encourage them, and even, on occasion, agree with them." She smirked, and he slowly returned her smile.

He opened his mouth to speak, but she lifted her hand. "No. I rejected you once, and I would never expect any man of dignity to ask a second time." At his puzzled look, she smiled again, rose, crossed the room, and, kneeling before him, took his hands in hers. His expression of shock nearly made her laugh, but she kept her composure. Looking directly into his eyes, she said, "Mr Watson—nay, Robert—I love you deeply and do not want to consider my life without you in it. Will you do me the great honour of becoming my husband? Will you marry me?"

Before she could say more, Robert was kneeling beside her, cupping her face and drawing her into a deep, passionate kiss. Her mind went utterly blank; she realised she had never known what it was to kiss someone who truly respected, valued, and loved her—and whom she loved in return. They might have stayed thus much longer had not a knock sounded at the door.

They scrambled to their feet, smoothing out creases in their clothing, just as Henry and Charles entered. The two men cast them knowing glances, and Henry said, "Well, my dear Watson, I do hope you have some news for me—otherwise I shall be very sad to have to call you out." Charles burst into laughter, and, receiving an irritated look from Henry, beat a hasty retreat back into the hall.

Robert and Cassandra, both beaming, informed Henry of their engagement and their wish to marry as soon as possible. Their families' happiness was only second to their own. Henry and Charles, delighted to see two such deserving people united, were equally pleased to think their households would at last be closely connected. Mrs Willoughby, who had remained in the hall in order to allow the men their fun, now joined them to add her congratulations as well.

Robert continued the tour of his home with new enthusiasm, knowing that the woman he loved would soon be mistress of all he had.

Epilogue

Robert and Cassandra married on the 25th of December 1770, having waited until all of their family could come together to celebrate their nuptials. They had determined to be the happiest of couples and to read to each other every day of their shared lives until death should part them.

Since she had never conceived during her previous marriage, they were both surprised and overjoyed when Cassandra felt the quickening within four months of their wedding. In late September of the following year, they welcomed their first child, whom they named Robert Willoughby Watson. Both Henry and Charles insisted on being godfathers' to the Watson's first child. Robbie Junior would later form a strong friendship with his cousin Charles Junior who was born two years later in January 1773 as Mr Charles Turner had remarried a month after little Robbie's first birthday.

In November of that same year, the Watsons christened their second child, Elizabeth Theophila Watson. Mrs Garforth, Mr and Mrs Hodgson, and Mr John Mordaunt, Robert's former brother-in-law all agreed to take up the roles of her godparents—though little Lizzy's second name was given in honour and memory of Mr Watson's late sister who had also been Mr Mordaunt's late wife. Elizabeth was followed two years later by Penelope Antonina Watson, born in mid-March. This time, Mr and Mrs Parker stood up along with Mr and Mrs Hewgill as the godparents to the young girl.

Believing their family complete, Mr and Mrs Watson were delighted with their children. However, three years after Penny, Margaret Arabella Watson was born in early April. This time, Robert's youngest sister Margaret—now Mrs Turner having married in '74—and her husband, Mr Turner—of the Turners of Oxfordshire—were asked to be godparents along with Mr and Mrs Francis Willoughby. When they were questioned about the choice of Maggie's second name, the two only smiled at each other as they remembered that long ago rainy day in Henry's library when Cassandra first read *The Female Quixote* to her dear Robert.

They were surprised when Maggie was followed two years later by Samuel Charles Watson in mid-December. The Reverend Mr Charles Mordaunt, younger brother of John, agreed to be one of the godparents and travelled to Yorkshire for the Christening. It was a memorable event as Sam had been born on the same day as his cousin, Henry Willoughby. The Reverend James Willoughby and his wife, Eleanor whom he had married two years after the Watsons wedding, had two little girls, but they had already lost two sons; one having passed away in February of that same year at just eight months old. They hoped the double birth was a good sign, and they had readily agreed to share in the duty of being Sam's godparents should the Watson's agree to the same for their dear little Henry. And so, the two boys were christened in the same ceremony with the whole Willoughby brood present to pray for both young men to live long and healthy lives. And, while it is not part of this story, the author is glad to tell you that their hopes were answered.

Their last little "blessing", as Cassandra liked to call their children, was named Emma Cassandra Watson. She entered the world two years after Sam, just shy of Maggie's fourth birthday, when Cassandra was forty-three. Mr Watson often jested that he was "glad that he had married a woman with so many relations as they would never have to worry about running out of godparents." Young William Garforth was now all grown up and had married a few days after the birth of Margaret which caused Mr and Mrs Watson to miss his wedding. However, the couple was asked and agreed to become godparents for little Emma in addition to Miss Dorothy Mordaunt, who at nearly sixty was still spry. Her inclusion was suggested by Mrs Parker who insisted that her aunt "would do as well as anyone else and had more to offer than most." While the Watsons assured Miss

Mordaunt that they had no expectations, she agreed—finding humour in the proposal.

The only shadow over Emma's Christening was that, Mrs Hodgson, having passed away the year before, was unable to be there to meet her namesake. Mr Hodgson assured Cassandra that his late-wife would have adored Emma just as she had all the rest. The Hodgsons had been childless, and Mrs Hodgson had doted on all her nieces and nephews as if they made up for that emptiness in her own life. Another downside of the timing of Mrs Hodgson's death was that she was unable to live long enough to see her brother, Henry, inherit the title Baron Middleton upon their cousins dying without male heirs.

Less than one month after Emma's birth, Mr Charles Turner—who had inherited the family's estate on the passing of his father in '74—was created a Baronet. He claimed that he needed to "keep up with his good friend as much as possible."

Though both his godparents attained titles, little Robbie Watson was never aware of what good connections he truly held—at least not until both of his godfathers had left the mortal coil, but that is a story for another day.

Before You Go

Did You Enjoy This Prequel?

If you enjoyed *The Watsons: Beginnings: Arc One: Courtship & Marriage*, don't miss the rest of the series.

Continue reading about the adventures of the Watson family in ***Refined and Returned**:* A Completed Version of *The Watsons* by Jane Austen in three Volumes by Eireanne Michaels.

Volume I

Available on Amazon, Draft2Digital, and associated retailers

You can also subscribe to my newsletter to be kept up to date on new releases and book or chapter previews at **Jane Austen's Literary Lasagna**.

https://jaliterarylasagna.wixsite.com/jane-austen-fandom

Preview

The Watsons Beginnings

Arc 2: Fortune & Family

England, summer, 1787.

Long before the events of Jane Austen's The Watsons, a simple offer redefined Emma Watson's entire life.

Seventeen years into Mrs Watsons second marriage, Mr and Mrs Edward Turner—Mr Watson's youngest half-sister and her husband—visited the Watson family with a proposal. Married for over a decade themselves without children of their own, the Turners decided to take in one of the Watson children to raise as their heir. With children in abundance and very little money to benefit them, Mr and Mrs Watson were eventually convinced to give up one of theirs to the cause. Reluctant though they were to part with any of their "little blessings", the Watsons ultimately agreed, recognizing the advantages the arrangement would provide for the chosen child.

Therefore, at just five years old, Emma Watson was taken away from the only home she had ever known, and her parents were left to bear the grief of her loss—a grief born not of death, but of their own inability to provide.

This is a story of family love and difficult choices. It is a pivotal chapter in the Watsons' history that shapes who they become, revealing both their love for their children and the sacrifices parents sometimes have to make for them.

Author Bio

Eireanne Michaels is an introvert who is currently living in Korea among some of her rescue cats. She is one of those women who is perfectly happy to be considered a 'crazy cat lady' as it both keeps people away and is simply the unavoidable truth.

She is a fan of fantasy, science fiction, and old British literature. She has been a fan of Jane Austen's novels for many, many years (possibly 'since tigers were smoking' which is the Korean way to say 'since dinosaurs roamed the earth.')

To Eireanne, Austen's works are like good lasagna; it's full of layers that bring new delicious titbits to the surface each time they are reached. However, most people only notice the toppings and miss the real meat underneath. Jane Austen was not just a great author; she had depths that we may never fully discover. It has created a passion, or possibly obsession, in this author to uncover all of the hidden gems in her sarcastic and witty novels by slowly dissecting them and, occasionally, reimagining them.

So, for her own amusement, she has decided to take up writing JAFF in order to help her better understand the time period, the characters, and the original author. While she writes for herself, she knows that there are others who are interested in the many facets of Austen's works who might also enjoy her works, and she decided to share them.

Thank you for reading!

www.ingramcontent.com/pod-product-compliance
Lightning Source LLC
LaVergne TN
LVHW050941080826
845145LV00004B/1356

* 9 7 8 1 9 6 9 8 4 1 0 4 0 *